Baby rabbits are called kittens.

Rabbits can see almost all round them.

They often live on railway banks.

Owls can see in the dark.

Foxes often hunt rabbits.

Females are called does, and males are called bucks.

A rabbit's home is called a warren.

Rabbits often run in a
zig-zag way.

Rabbits sniff the air all the time.

Badgers come out at night.

When it's safe, rabbits like
to sunbathe!

Sometimes, rabbits grunt softly
when they are pleased.

A catalogue record for this book is available from the British Library

Published by Ladybird Books Ltd Loughborough Leicestershire UK
Ladybird Books Ltd is a subsidiary of the Penguin Group of companies
© LADYBIRD BOOKS LTD MCMXCVI
LADYBIRD and the device of a Ladybird are trademarks of Ladybird Books Ltd

The Great Rabbit Race

by Geraldine Taylor
illustrated by Lesley Smith

Picture Ladybird

"I want to see what's *outside*," said the little brown rabbit; "we've been up and down every tunnel in this warren. Let's go *outside*…" He crept towards the bright light and two other little brown rabbits followed. Their little grey sister held back. She remembered that their mother had warned them never, *absolutely never,* to go outside without her…

Suddenly their mother appeared, large and cross.

"Listen to me, little rabbits. Outside is a big, thrilling place – but it's dangerous and you must obey the rules. *Never* go outside alone – not until you've earned your grown-up names."

Little grey rabbit twitched her ears in excitement and wondered what *her* grown-up name would be.

"There's a lot to learn first," said her mother. "Line up, don't dawdle, follow me – we're going outside."

On the warm grass outside the warren, Mother Rabbit watched her little rabbits race each other up and down the bank, their white tails bobbing. Then she taught them to sniff the air, to sit up on their back legs to look around – and to listen with their long ears for the faintest sounds from far away.

"And if you hear *this* noise, little rabbits," she said, "there's *danger* outside and you must race home as fast as you can." She lifted one of her long back feet and hit the ground with a loud, hollow thump.

"Now," she said, "say your rabbit drill –
        Sniff and listen,
        Look around,
        If there's danger, thump the ground.
        Then run, rabbits, RUN…"

Free to explore while her mother watched, little grey rabbit gave two excited jumps for joy, dashed in circles and tumbled down the bank. Her three brothers raced after her and then all four rabbits stopped as still as stones, sat up and peeped into a huge black hole.

"That," said little grey rabbit, "is an *enormous* rabbit hole."

"*Giant* rabbits live there," said one of her brothers. "Look – something's coming – it's..."

But no one could hear him. A long, shining and deafening creature shot out of the giant hole and roared along a gleaming path. The three brown rabbits were frozen with fear, but little grey rabbit turned and ran like the wind back to her mother.

"I've seen danger! Danger's down there!" she cried.

"Little rabbits," said their mother, "that's a *train*. Keep well away. But it's not the train you've to run from. It's the red shape watching the train. That's the *fox*. Always run from the fox."

"I smelt the fox!" said one of the little brown rabbits. "It was *horrible*."

"That's true," said his mother. "Your grown-up name is Sharp Nose. You will warn us about foxes."

Four little rabbits danced in the sunlight while far away, and hidden, the fox sat watching.

That night, their mother led the little rabbits outside again and they tiptoed cautiously into the darkness.

As little grey rabbit looked up at the sky, black clouds parted and an enormous white face frowned down at her.

She ran like the wind to her mother.

"I've seen danger! Danger's up there!"

"Little rabbits," said their mother, "That's the *moon*. It's not the moon you've to run from. It's the dark wings that cross the moon. That's the *owl*. Always hide from the owl."

"I heard the owl crying," said one of the little brown rabbits.

"That's true," said his mother. "Owls cry in the night. Your grown-up name is Sharp Ears. You will warn us about owls."

"And I saw something move in the woods…"
said his brother. "It was black and white…"

"That was a *badger*," said his mother. "Badgers
wear the colours of moonlight. Never trust
badgers. Your grown-up name, little rabbit,
is Sharp Eyes. You will warn
us about badgers."

Little grey rabbit felt silly. She had been running too fast to hear the owl or see the badger – but she wanted her grown-up name, too.

Four little rabbits stared at the stars while far away, and hidden, the fox sat watching.

One morning, as the stars faded and the clouds turned pink, the little rabbits raced, and practised their rabbit drill. Then, while their mother watched, they crept close to the giant train tunnel, where the grass and dandelions grew thickly.

Suddenly, the ground shook and an enormous train roared from the tunnel.

As it thundered along, little grey rabbit thought she heard it saying – *Little rabbit, what's your name? Little rabbit, what's your name?*

"I want my name. I'm going to ask my mother for *my* name!" said the little grey rabbit…

And she turned to run back to her mother at the top of the bank.

But she stopped.

Sharp Nose said, "I can smell the fox…"

Sharp Ears said, "Listen – someone's thumping…"

Sharp Eyes said, "Look – our mother's thumping the ground…"

All four rabbits cried, "It's the *fox*…"

The fox was waiting… between them and their warren.

"*Race* me home..." cried little grey rabbit.
"Run, rabbits, RUN..."
She thumped the ground to give herself
courage – then she ran like the wind!

Her brothers thumped the ground, too, and
raced after little grey rabbit straight towards
the fox!

When she had almost reached him, little grey rabbit darted to one side, then the other. Her brothers also zig-zagged from one side to the other behind her.

The fox lunged after little grey rabbit – but she darted away. He lunged after Sharp Eyes – and *he* changed direction, too.

The fox dashed angrily here and there and suddenly all four little rabbits were safely in the warren, hearts beating wildly.

When she saw that her little rabbits were safe, Mother Rabbit rushed down a hidden hole behind the warren to join them.

"What a great race!" said their mother, proudly. "Little grey rabbit, your grown-up name is Racer, and one day…"

But she stopped. Little grey rabbit was fast asleep – and yet her long back feet were twitching. Even in her dreams, Racer was running, ready for whatever adventure might happen next…

Mother rabbit sat down beside the little sleeping rabbit and whispered, "My name is Racer, too."

Race home with the rabbits!

INSTRUCTIONS FOR
THE GREAT RABBIT RACE GAME

How to Play

You will need:
A number die or a block with numbers 1-6 on it.
A differently coloured button or counter for each player.

All rabbits begin at the tunnel marked START.

Take it in turns to throw the die and move your counter
the same number of squares as the number on the die.

If you land on a RUN square – have another throw.

If you land on the STOP AND LOOK, LISTEN, SNIFF or
THUMP square – stop and miss a turn.

If you land on the STOP TO NIBBLE DANDELION
square – go back two squares.

You've landed on the FOX square! Go forward two
squares and follow the racing short cut to the warren.

Badger Wood

Railway Tunnel

Dandelion
Patch

RUN!
HAVE ANOTHER
THROW.

RUN!
HAVE ANOTHER
THROW.

START

FINISH

Rabbits' Warren

RUN THIS WAY...

Sunny Meadow

Owl Tree

RUN-OWL!
THROW AGAIN.

RUN.
THROW AGAIN.

STOP
AND LISTEN.
MISS A GO.

Picture Ladybird
Books for reading aloud with 2 – 6 year olds

The exciting *Picture Ladybird* series includes a wide range of animal stories, funny rhymes, and real life adventures that are perfect to read aloud and share at storytime or bedtime.

A whole library of beautiful books for you to collect

RHYMING STORIES
Easy to follow and great for joining in!

Jasper's Jungle Journey, Val Biro
Shoo Fly, Shoo! Brian Moses
Ten Tall Giraffes, Brian Moses
In Comes the Tide, Valerie King
Toot! Learns to Fly,
Geraldine Taylor & Jill Harker
Who Am I? Judith Nicholls
Fly Eagle, Fly! Jan Pollard

IMAGINATIVE TALES
Mysterious and magical, or just a little shivery

The Star that Fell, Karen Hayles
Wishing Moon, Lesley Harker
Don't Worry William, Christine Morton
This Way Little Badger, Phil McMylor
The Giant Walks, Judith Nicholls
Kelly and the Mermaid, Karen King

FUNNY STORIES
Make storytime good fun!

Benedict Goes to the Beach, Chris Demarest
Bella and Gertie, Geraldine Taylor
Edward Goes Exploring, David Pace
Telephone Ted, Joan Stimson
Top Shelf Ted, Joan Stimson
Helpful Henry, Shen Roddie
What's Wrong with Bertie? Tony Bradman
Bears Can't Fly, Val Biro
Finnigan's Flap, Joan Stimson

REAL LIFE ADVENTURE
Situations to explore and discover

Joe and the Farm Goose,
Geraldine Taylor & Jill Harker
Going to Playgroup,
Geraldine Taylor & Jill Harker
The Great Rabbit Race, Geraldine Taylor
Pushchair Polly, Tony Bradman